We're All in the SAME BOAT

ZACHARY SHAPIRO   Illustrated by JACK E. DAVIS

G. P. Putnam's Sons

It rained and it rained.
It rained so much that Noah had to build
an ark to protect all the animals.

At first the animals were excited about their trip.
"A few days at sea sounds so thrilling!"
they said to one another.

But the days turned into weeks.
And the weeks turned into months.
And the animals were getting restless.

The ants were antsy.
The bees were bored.

The camels were complaining.

The dogs were demanding.

The elephants were **enraged**.

The **f**oxes were **f**rantic.

The **g**iraffes were **g**rumpy.

The **h**yenas were **h**ysterical.

The oXen were eXasperated.

The yaks were **yelling**.

The zebras were zoned-out.

And they all blamed Noah.

And Noah took
a deep breath
and hollered—

For the first time, there was silence.
And then, a funny thing began to happen. . . .

The **a**nts **a**pologized
and the **b**ees **b**ehaved.

The **c**amels were **c**ooperative,

the **d**ogs were
diligent,

and the **e**lephants were **en**thusiastic.

The **f**oxes told **f**ables
and the **g**iraffes
made **g**ifts.

The **h**yenas were still

hysterical.

The iguanas invited the jaguars to jam.

The kangaroos
played kickball
while the
llamas laughed.

The **m**oose were **m**erry
and the **n**ightingales
were **n**eighborly.
The **o**rangutans **o**rganized their toys.

The penguins held a party
where the quails quoted rhymes with the rabbits.

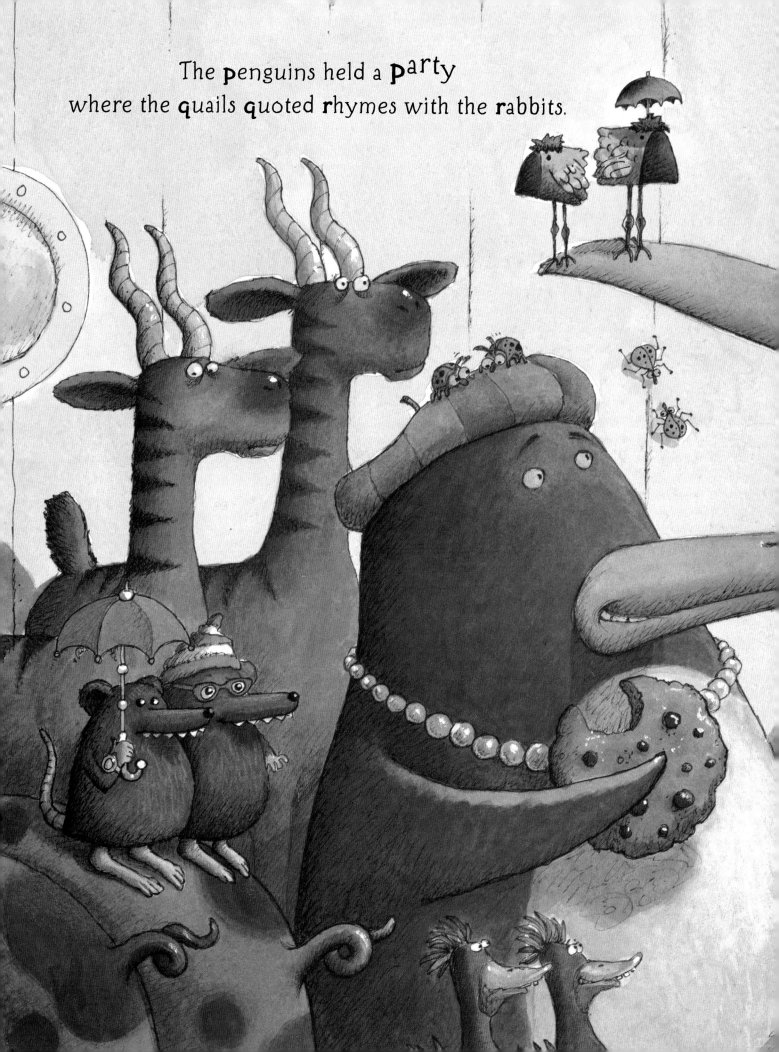

The snakes **s**tretched.

The **t**oads were **t**uckered out.

The **u**mbrella birds **u**prighted themselves.
The **v**oles **v**olunteered to
keep **w**atch with the **w**orms.

The oXen were eXhausted.
The yaks began to yawn.

The **zebras** crawled into bed to catch their **zzzzz**'s.

And as Noah tucked his animals in for the night,
the ark sailed on with a promise of peace.

For Grandma Anne and Grandpa Phil, who taught me to tell stories. And for Ron, who inspired me to write.—Z. S.

For Johnny, Michael, Jaso and Pudge.—J. E. D.

G. P. PUTNAM'S SONS. A division of Penguin Young Readers Group. Published by The Penguin Group. Penguin Group (USA) Inc., 375 Hudson Street, New York, NY 10014, U.S.A. Penguin Group (Canada), 90 Eglinton Avenue East, Suite 700, Toronto, Ontario M4P 2Y3, Canada (a division of Pearson Penguin Canada Inc.). Penguin Books Ltd, 80 Strand, London WC2R 0RL, England. Penguin Ireland, 25 St. Stephen's Green, Dublin 2, Ireland (a division of Penguin Books Ltd.). Penguin Group (Australia), 250 Camberwell Road, Camberwell, Victoria 3124, Australia (a division of Pearson Australia Group Pty Ltd). Penguin Books India Pvt Ltd, 11 Community Centre, Panchsheel Park, New Delhi - 110 017, India. Penguin Group (NZ), 67 Apollo Drive, Rosedale, North Shore 0632, New Zealand (a division of Pearson New Zealand Ltd). Penguin Books (South Africa) (Pty) Ltd, 24 Sturdee Avenue, Rosebank, Johannesburg 2196, South Africa. Penguin Books Ltd, Registered Offices: 80 Strand, London WC2R 0RL, England.

Library of Congress Cataloging-in-Publication Data. Shapiro, Zachary. We're all in the same boat / Zachary Shapiro ; illustrated by Jack E. Davis. p. cm. Summary: After being on the ark for months and months, the ants get antsy, the bees bored, and the llamas livid, and Noah must find a way to make everyone get along. [1. Noah's ark—Fiction. 2. Animals—Fiction. 3. Behavior—Fiction. 4. Alphabet.] I. Davis, Jack E., ill. II. Title. III. Title: We are all in the same boat. PZ7.S52959We 2008 [E]—dc22
2007041316 ISBN 978-0-399-24393-6 10 9 8 7 6 5 4 3 2